MW00509037

EXPLICIT
EROTIC SEX STORIES

The great Biker Fantasy, Road to Unknown – Steamy and Lascivious Biker Fantasy Erotic Story

By **Julia Saint**

I was standing on Mount Lemmon looking out over the desert at the lights of Tucson that night.

The night that turned my whole damn life into one wild ride.

I was bored. Tired of my job, tired of my now ex-girlfriend. Tired of life in general.

The only thing that was going right for me was my Hawg. A 1956 Harley-Davidson Panhead.

It's not often that a person can look back on a moment and say, "there, that is where I made the choice that turned my life upside-down".

In my case, it was when I decided to go sit on a big boulder and watch the storm coming across the city from the south.

I had an ideal perch from which to watch the light show as the thunderstorm flowed up the valley from Nogales. I fished around in my pocket for my pipe and my tobacco pouch. I filled my pipe and lit it. At peace with the world for once, I settled cross-legged on the more or less flat top of the boulder and cleared my mind. I had tried this type of meditation before, and it usually helped to relax me. I puffed the pipe evenly and slowly, letting the tension flow out with the smoke.

Finally I was relaxed as I was going to get. I stayed there for hours, not moving except to refill my pipe and relight it. When I climbed down off the boulder a few hours before dawn, I felt as if I had been asleep for days.

I stopped before going back to the bike and pissed off the edge of the cliff. When I got back to my bike though, I noticed something was more than a little odd. I could have sworn that the road that I had driven up on had been paved. But all I saw was gravel road, heavily rutted and badly in need of repair. I shrugged it off. I had been over worse roads before.

I kicked the Harley to life easily. Letting her warm up for a bit before I dropped her in gear and started out. Being a rigid frame bike, my Harley damn near bounced my kidneys loose by the time I got down the mountain. The sun was just coming up by the time I got to the main road, or where the main road should have been anyway.

I KNEW that Camino Seco was paved. But all I found was another rutted dirt road, maybe a little wider than the one I had just come off of. And where the hell were the buildings that were part of Tucson's urban sprawl? I could see nothing but cactus, mesquite, and Palo Verde everywhere I looked.

I headed west towards town. I rode for a good hour without seeing a single person. Hell, for that matter, I hadn't seen a frigging house or any other sign of civilization. I kept heading generally southwest towards where I knew downtown Tucson was supposed to be. I had a few bad moments crossing rickety bridges across dry washes. But no major trouble. I was getting seriously worried though.

I was thirsty, and no water in sight. I stopped when I saw the next good-sized barrel cactus. The Bowie knife from my boot made short work of chopping the top of the cactus open. I dipped out the watery pulp inside and gulped it down, nasty tasting stuff. But it stayed down and gave me the moisture I needed. I made myself drink as much as I could hold. Then replaced the top of the cactus and got back on the bike.

I unscrewed the gas cap and checked the fuel. 3/4 full, enough to get me to Nogales if I had to.

I was puzzled, someone had to be maintaining these roads, such as they were. But who? And where the hell were they?

I kept going, hoping for some sign that someone was here. When I reached A Mountain, I knew I was screwed. No big white A picked out in white rocks. And where I was sitting should have been right downtown in Tucson.

Crap and other comments.

I reached into the saddlebags behind the seat of the bike and pulled out my pistol and gun belt. I had a sinking feeling that I would need the firepower of my .44 mag before much longer. I stopped and considered my options. Going back up the mountain had its appeal, but I was just stubborn enough to try to make it down to Nogales.

In the Tucson that I knew, it was a simple drive of maybe an hour to the border. Now? I wasn't sure. I found a road heading generally south and took it.

I was somewhere around where I expected Tubac to be, and still nothing and no one. This was not good.

I could see the storm clouds gathering ahead of me. Good old reliable monsoons. At least that hadn't changed.

I found a spot on a little hill and dug my tarp out of my duffle bag. I rigged it between a couple of Palo Verde trees and a couple of poles that I cut with my Bowie knife. I sank the poles a good 3 feet into the ground, then lashed the tarp to them and guyed cords out to big rocks to help keep them upright.

Safe enough from the rain, I rigged a plastic drop cloth to act as a rain catcher. If we got enough rain, I could fill my canteens and my water bag. I didn't bother with a fire, I didn't have anything to cook, and nothing to cook in if I did. I munched one of the granola bars that I always kept in my saddlebags. I sat backwards on my bike, my head cushioned by my duffle bag, and my feet crossed on the rear fender. I watched the storm roll in and over me, lightning flashing and the rain coming down like a cow pissing on a flat rock.

The plastic drop cloth held a good 3 or 4 gallons when the rain stopped. I filled the canteens and the water bag first. Then I drank my fill of the clean, cold water.

I left the tarp up and leaned back on the bike again. I had slept on the back of the Harley many times, so this was nothing new.

When I woke up, I sat up and stretched. I had slept a lot better than I had expected. I went to take the tarp down. I took a step towards the trees and stopped. "What the fuck?" I said aloud. I had lived in Tucson for 14 goddamn years. I know Palo Verde trees when I see them. And I had tied the tarp to a couple of Palo Verde trees. Now it was tied to a couple of small oaks. I turned and looked out at the surrounding area. Grasslands dotted with small groves of trees.

I took the tarp down and stowed it. then drank the last of the water from the plastic sheet. I got everything packed and got on the bike. She started easily and idled smoothly, or at least, as smoothly as any Harley does. I idled for a few minutes, then shut the bike down. I checked the oil and the tire pressure. Both good. I adjusted the chain slightly and then restarted the bike.

The road I had been traveling on was gone. No trace at all. But the grass was short, and the ground firm enough for traction, so I continued on south. There were mountains in the distance in a couple of directions, but they weren't the same mountains that could be seen from Tucson.

I kept going south because I was already pointed in that direction, and it was as good as any other direction at the moment.

I kept the speed low, no more than 30 miles per hour at any time, both to conserve fuel, and to avoid any sudden surprises like unseen drop-offs or big bike eating rocks.

After an hour or so, I finally saw someone.

Several some-ones actually. I had stopped up on top of a hill and shut off the bike to get a look at the surrounding land, hoping to see a town or even a herd of animals. The grass was too uniformly short to be ungrazed, and I had seen piles of dung that looked like the cow chips that I remembered from my West Nebraska boyhood.

I saw something moving out a mile or so away. I dug in my duffle bag and got out my old battered binoculars. I looked through the side that had the uncracked lens. There were several guys on horses chasing a woman or girl who was on foot. She had a good lead on them, but it was shrinking fast.

I fired up the Harley and headed in that direction. The men on horseback either didn't hear me, or just ignored me as I approached. The girl looked up when she heard the big V Twin of the Hawg, then tripped and fell.

I was close enough to see that the horsemen had lances and swords. They wore leather armor with small brass studs all over the leather. I didn't know why they were chasing the girl, but I have always been a sucker for the underdog.

I drove my bike through the group of horsemen, revving the engine and scaring the shit out of the horses. By the time the riders got their mounts under control, I had the Bike stopped next to the girl on the ground. I spared her a quick glance. He bare feet were bloody and her dress was torn and ragged. She herself looked filthy. I couldn't tell much else since she had her face hidden in her arms as she lay face down.

I drew my .44 pointed it straight up. "All right, that's far enough!" I yelled at the horsemen. Most of them drew up and stopped. One of them, maybe a little braver, or stupider, than the others, kept coming. He dropped his lance point even with my chest and spurred his horse. I took a two handed grip on the .44 and fired.

I remembered reading something about fighting cavalry, kill the horse, and the rider is easy meat.

So the horse took the first 240-grain hollow-point right in the forehead. Momentum carried it a few feet further, but it was already dead and dropping. The rider broke his neck when he landed with an audible SNAP! The rest of the men milled their horses around. Then one of then shouted something at me in a language I had never heard. "Sprechen se Deutch?" I tried. Nothing. "Parles vous Francais?" Again nada. ""Que Pasa?" Again nothing. I thought hard, "Hoka Hey," Again just puzzled expressions.

One of the men rode forward slowly. When he was still a few yards away, I held up my left hand palm out. I kept the gun trained on him. He understood the gesture and stopped his horse as if he had run into a wall. He gestured at his fallen companion and said something in a pleading tone. I raised the muzzle of the pistol and waved my hand to tell him to go ahead.

The man dismounted and walked over to the dead man. He knelt by the corpse and checked for a pulse. I knew there wouldn't be one, the dead dude's head was damn near torn off.

The man went and looked at the shattered skull of the dead horse, then walked back to his mount.

The man then did something that surprised me. He took off his sword belt and hung it on his saddlebow. He divested himself of a surprising array of cutlery, daggers, knives, etc. even something suspiciously like a shuriken throwing star. If I had known he had those damn things, He would never have gotten that close.

He turned and yelled something at the others, and they jabbed their lances point first into the ground and dismounted.

The closer man held his hands out to show that they were empty and started slowly forward. I holstered the .44 and put the kickstand down on the bike. I stepped off and moved away from the Harley. Making sure that I kept myself and the bike between the men and the girl. She was still lying down, shaking and sobbing.

The rider stopped an arms length from me. He looked me up and down, taking in my red and white beard, my long blonde and white ponytail. I had on my leathers and a black T-shirt with a picture of a wizard shooting lightning from his fingertips over a group of skeletal bikers. I had bought that shirt at a truck stop in New Mexico. I had several more in my duffle bag.

Up close, the man reeked of old sweat and stale piss. Doubtless I didn't smell much better after a desert ride in my heavy leathers.

The rider was clean-shaven, about 30 with short dark hair and a nasty scar on his face. ""In Nomine, Padre, et Fili, Et Espiritu Sanctu." I said. The man shrugged and smiled, showing several broken teeth.

The girl picked this time to sit up and make herself visible again.

I saw the look in the riders face as he saw the girl and his expression changed. I stepped back warily and tossed a glance over my shoulder. The girl was peeking over the seat of the Harley, her long brown hair blowing in the breeze.

I turned my attention back to the rider. He pointed at her and shouted. I stood there until he ran down and then shook my head no. The man grew even angrier and stomped his foot, looking for all the world like a kid having a tantrum.

I suppose I shouldn't have laughed at him, but I just couldn't help it.

The rider spat on the ground at my feet, then spun and stomped back to his horse. "Hey buddy!" I yelled at him as he swung into the saddle. He turned and glared at me, so I gave him a one-finger salute and suggested that his father was into bestiality.

He may not have understood the language, but he caught the insulting tone. The rider got back to his buddies and waited for them to mount up.

I drew the .44 and reloaded the spent chamber. 5 of them, 6 shots for me. I liked the odds.

As soon as the brave one raised his sword, I shot him. At 50 yards, I shot for the horse, and missed high. The bullet meant for the horse hit the rider at the base of the throat and damn near beheaded him. I corrected my aim and brought down the other horses as fast as I could sight and pull the trigger.

I flipped open the cylinder and dumped the empty brass as I reached for a speed loader. Only one of the horsemen had regained his feet by the time I was reloaded. I started walking swiftly towards them, holding my fire until I was closer.

Only 3 were still able to stand when I got within 30 feet of them, and at that range, I didn't miss. The down and injured riders I finished off with their own lances. I didn't want to waste any ammo that I didn't have to.

I scavenged the knives, swords etc. from the corpses. I searched for money, but only found small metal bars about a finger long and wide in their belt pouches, so I took them along.

One horse was still standing, and that only because his reins were still clutched in the dead hand of his rider. I pulled the reins loose and led the horse back to the bike. The girl stood up and I got a better look at her. About 5'3", slender and small busted, she looked to be in her early to mid teens. I handed her the reins of the horse. At first she shied away from taking them, but I took her hand and closed her fingers around the leather. She took a step and winced. I cursed myself for not remembering her feet.

I picked her up and sat her sideways on my bike. I tied the reins to the sissy bar and fished my first aid kit out of the duffle bag.
I dug out a box of ammo for the .44 and reloaded the speed loader and the cylinder before I did anything else. I put the empty brass in the box for possible later reloading. When I ran out of ammo for the magnum, I was screwed.

I then used water from the water bag to wash the girls feet before treating them. She trembled at my touch, but did not try to pull away. The soles of her feet were lacerated, but none of the wounds were deep. I slathered them with antibiotic ointment and wrapped them snugly in gauze bandages. I had a pair of socks in the duffle bag, and I got them out and worked them on over her feet.

I went back to the dead men and cut the leather inner shirt off one of them. I brought it back to her and sliced and sewed the shirt into a serviceable pair of moccasins to protect her bandages.

I examined her further and found other minor wounds and treated them. I managed to get her to swallow a couple of aspirin and a couple of vitamin pills. She made a face at the taste, but otherwise cooperated.

Her dress was an unholy mess, so I dug out one of my T-shirts. This one had a beautiful dragon on the front. I cut away the top of her dress and sewed the skirt to the T-shirt. She had made a halfhearted objection when I had cut away her blouse, but she had relaxed when I pulled the shirt over her head and started sewing.

It was getting late and I was thinking about shelter. The girl picked up one of the knives and made her way over to one of the dead horses. She was still limping, but had little trouble cutting out a couple of nice chunks of meat and bringing them back to me in one of the dead men's saddlebags.

I helped her up onto the horse and gestured for her to lead the way. I started the bike and followed slowly.

The girl led me to a ring of standing stones a few miles away. The first thing I thought was 'Stonehenge" But there were only superficial resemblances. I had seen the real Stonehenge during my time in the Army, and this place had a much different feel.

I dug a small hole and built a small fire in it, propping the chucks of horsemeat over the fire on green sticks. While the meat cooked, I went to the altar stone and examined it. On a sudden impulse, I put a few of the metal bars on the altar, and I added a few coins from my own pocket.

The girl watched me as I stood there. I made a small cut on my finger and let a couple of drops fall on the stone.
The girl gasped, but when I looked at her, her face gave nothing away. I went over and cut a piece of the meat and put it on the altar, sprinkling it with some salt from a packet that I had kept from a fast food joint.

When I went back and sat down, the girl scooted over and sat next to me. I gave her a couple of packets of salt and pepper, then got out a couple for me. The girl looked at me confused, then followed suit when I opened mine and sprinkled it over the chunks of meat.

The meat was finally done enough, and the girl and I dug in.

I wiped the grease from her chin with my bandanna. She gave me a shy smile and went back to eating. She finished her portion and the last half of mine. I washed up and then made her stay still while I cleaned her face and hands.

Clean, she was actually very pretty, and looked about 14. Boy was I off by a few decades... I spread out my bedroll, then went out of the stone ring to a small grove a few yards off to leak and take a dump. When I got back, the girl was in my bedding, and her clothing was neatly laid out beside it. I sighed, not that I wasn't flattered, but I was just too damn tired.

I sat down and took off my boots, then I took off the jacket and shirt, I figured that my old clothes badly needed a good airing. I shed my jeans and boxers, then slid into the blankets with my gun and Bowie next to my head. I turned onto my side and felt the girl snuggle up to my back and put an arm around me. I was asleep in moments. Just before I went under, the thought occurred to me that I might wake up in yet another place and time, but since I couldn't do a thing about it...

In the morning, the girl and the stone rings were still there. The Harley was still parked a few feet away, and the ashes in the fire pit steamed gently from the dew.

There was a thick fog everywhere but inside the ring. Sounds were strangely muffled and the hairs on the back of my neck were standing on end. I slipped out of the blankets and pulled fresh pants, socks and a shirt out of the duffle bag. I dressed quickly and stomped into my boots. I sheathed the knife and slung my gun belt around my waist and buckled it. I checked the loads in the cylinder and re-holstered the gun. When I looked around, the girl was dressed and lacing on her makeshift moccasins. I felt a sting on my shoulder and rubbed it. I could feet two small punctures near my neck.

"What the fuck?" I said. I looked back at the girl. "What the hell are you? A goddamn vampire?"
She looked up at me. "Not quite." "So you do speak my language." I said.

"Not until last night." She said calmly. "I needed to connect with you to join minds long enough to learn to communicate with you."

"So you bit me on the frigging neck?"

"Well, you did not accept the other form of connection offered." She said with a sly smile.

Great, I pass up a piece of ass, trying to be a gentleman, and what do I get? Fangs in my neck.

I parked my butt on the seat of the bike. "So just what are you?"

"I am one of the Free Folk."

"Free Folk, right." I said. "And just why were the jokers on horseback chasing you?"

The girl looked down at her feet. "One of the men thought I was a simple village girl and decided that he wanted me. When I objected, he tried to rape me. I killed him."

"So who were they? Soldiers?"

The girl spat. "A band of mercenaries out for whatever they could get."

"My name is Bill." I said. "What's yours?"

She was silent for a long time. "The way I see it, you owe me the courtesy of telling me your name." I said.

The girl glanced nervously at the altar stone. The coins and meat were gone. She took a deep breath and started to say something. She jumped as if stung, then looked like she was listening to a chewing out from someone, wincing now and then and looking as guilty as a kid with her hand in the cookie jar.

"My name is Jessie." She said at last.

"Can't lie around here huh?" I gibed.

She snarled at me. "Don't mock what you don't understand."

"No mockery intended." I assured her. "At least, not of any beings here that I cannot see. But you," and I fixed her with a glare of my own. "You are another story. I save your ass and you try to replay my kindness with bullshit and half truths." Jessie cringed at that. "I apologize." She said. "I am in your debt far more than you know."

I grinned at her. "No harm, No foul."

I made her sit on the bike again and unwrapped her feet. They already looked better. I put on more antibiotic ointment and put on new gauze. I laced her moccasins on again, a little more snugly this time.

"Do you know of a safe place to go?" I asked Jessie. "We need someplace to lay up for a few days to let you heal, and I need to figure out how to get fuel for my bike."

Jessie bit her lip, then nodded. "I know of a place, but it is about 30 miles from here, and the rest of the mercenaries will be out looking for their friend."

I just gave her an evil grin. "Not a problem." I told her. "But we'll be leaving the horse here."

She looked at me like I had 3 heads. "You want me to ride this thing?" she waved her hand at my bike.

"You and I will ride Cindy here," I told Jessie. "She's a hunk of old iron, but she's a lot more dependable than the bitch I named her after."

I showed Jessie where the rear foot pegs were. "We'll tuck up your skirts and you'll sit behind me and hold on to my waist."

Jessie grimaced. "If I must."

"As soon as the fog lifts, we'll go." I said.

Jessie glanced at the altar and then scrambled to put her feet on the proper pegs. "We have about 1 minute." She said.

I swung my leg over the bike and kicked her to life. As soon as the big V Twin roared, the fog vanished. Jessie pointed over my shoulder. "That way!" she cried.

I popped the clutch and we roared off down the slope in the direction she pointed. "Thanks!" I called back over my shoulder.

I raced across the flatlands at almost 60 miles an hour. I steered in the directions Jessie pointed out to me as we jounced along. I saw some horsemen off in the distance, but we were gone long before they got close enough to get a good look at us. I started seeing signs of habitation, cultivated fields etc. But I didn't see any people except at real long distances. I figured the sound of the Harley spooked them. I laughed aloud at that thought. Much the same thing happened back home when people heard the big V Twin talkin' at them.

Jessie was a good passenger, not trying to lean and just following my movements. I spotted a creek up ahead and to the right. I pulled over at a clump of trees near the water and shut down the bike. "Is this place safe to rest and maybe clean up a bit?" I asked my passenger.

"For now." Jessie said as she climbed down stiffly. "You ride this thing all the time?"

"Whenever possible." I shrugged as I started to undress. "Don't worry, you'll get used to it in time."

Jessie muttered something suspiciously like," Not if I can help it." But I ignored her while I fished a bar of soap from the duffle bag.

The water was cold as hell, but better than the gritty and grimy feel of several days without a shower or a bath.

My time in prison had gotten me used to showering every other day at least.
Jessie watched me swim around for a little, then gave into the temptation and stripped off her clothes and the bandages on her feet and dove off a rock into the pool of water. She surfaced near me, teeth chattering at the shock of the cold water. "Nice of you to join me." I smirked.

She splashed me. I turned her around and lathered her hair with the bar of soap. She sputtered a bit, but I just dunked her to rinse the soap out. After that, she just let me scrub her clean. We climbed out onto the bank and stretched out to let the sun and warm breeze dry us off.

I put on the old clothes again once I was dry, and Jessie dressed as well. I checked her feet, but they were healed enough that I just put my oversized socks and the moccasins back on her feet again.

Once back on the bike, Jessie pointed us in the right direction.

Another 30 minutes of riding found us traveling down a dirt road bordered by stone walls.

Farmhouses and cottages were everywhere now, but still only fleeting glimpses of people as the roar of the Harley echoed from the stone walls.

We wheeled into a town laid out much like those I had seen in Europe in my Army days.

I pulled into the town square and killed the engine. "Is this the place?" I asked Jessie.

"We can stop for a meal here, and to pick up supplies, but our destination is a few miles further along the east road."

"Where's the food?" I asked Jessie. She pointed at a building with a cup painted above the door.

"You might want to order for us." I told Jessie. "You might understand me, but I don't speak the lingo here."

"True." Jessie said as I lifted her from the Harley.

She led the way into the inn. We found a seat easily enough, the place was nearly deserted.

I gave Jessie a handful of the metal bars that apparently passed for money here. "This should cover our bill." I told her.

The innkeeper came over nervously, wiping his hands on his apron. Jessie chattered something at him, and he answered back sharply. Jessie turned to me. "he says he doesn't serve my kind in here." She said.

"Tell the tub of lard that I am not ordering one of your kind, and that if I don't see food on the table in two minutes, I'm gonna turn his fat ass into dog-meat."

Jessie looked at me, then turned to the innkeeper and repeated what I had said. The man paled, but stood firm.

"Tell the man that time is running out. And I am hungry and irritable." I said. "And if he does not start bringing food, I am sure his widow or heirs will be much more reasonable."

Jessie spoke to the man again, then tossed him a gold ingot. The innkeeper bit the metal and inspected the dents his teeth left.

Suddenly he was smiling and eager to please. Wooden mugs full of rather flat beer arrived within moments, followed seconds later by a platter of roast beef and a savory stew.

A girl I took to be the innkeeper's daughter brought out hot, steaming loaves of bread. Jessie and I at like a couple of starving wolves.

The beer may have been lousy, but the food was wonderful. I had Jessie tell the innkeeper that his cooks were the most talented I had come across in many years, and that the food was fit for the Gods. This made him preen and strut a bit, and he was definitely much friendlier.

Jessie and I decided to forgo buying supplies since our destination was so close.

Back on the road, we headed towards the nearby mountains. The surface of the road went from dirt and gravel to cobblestones, then to solid rock.

A few miles into the mountains, we came to a huge gate set in a wall that stretched from one side of the pass to the other. I stopped, and Jessie called up to the guard towers.

I didn't see anyone, but I figured that hidden bowmen from the arrow slits high above us were covering us. That's how I would have done it.

Whatever Jessie said to them, the gates creaked open. "Go ahead and pass through, do not stop until we are around the next bend in the road."

"Gotcha." I said. I let the clutch out and putted through the gate, then sped up slightly until we were well away from the gate. There was a second gate ahead, but it opened as well when my passenger stood on her foot pegs and shouted something.

I motored through that gate as well. A mile or so further, we passed through gates that were already open and into a city. People scattered as the Hawg's engine echoed off the stone walls of the buildings.

Jessie pointed over my shoulder and I swung off the street into the courtyard of an impressive building. I stopped near the marble steps leading to the big bronze doors. I put the kickstand down and got off the bike.

I lifted Jessie down and waited for her to make the next move.

"Bring the swords and booty from the mercenaries inside with us." She said.

I unstrapped the leather bundle from the sissy bar. I slung it over my left shoulder and we started up the steps.

As we approached the top of the stairs, the doors opened and a handsome man and a stunningly lovely woman came out. Jessie ran to them and hugged them both. I followed more slowly, the weight of all that metal on my shoulder was slowing me down.

"Come on inside." Jessie said gaily. The good-looking couple stepped aside to let us pass.

"Are these your parents?" I asked Jessie.

"Oh no," she laughed. "Marcus and Penelope are the heads of the household staff. They've been with us for ages."

"Well, who are we here to meet?" I asked. "My brother should be home. Our parents are away at our other home."

A youthful man came out of a side room and walked up to Jessie, holding out his hands to her. He barely gave me a glance until Jessie spoke to him. Then he looked me over carefully. He spoke to Jessie, but I didn't like the tone. She snapped back at him. Her brother raised his hand as if to slap her.

I wasn't aware I had moved until I saw the muzzle of the .44 pressing up under his chin. Jessie spoke to him rapidly and urgently. His face paled and he put both hands up in plain view. I uncocked the .44 and shoved it into the holster.

"Tell your brother that if he hits you, or even looks like he's going to, I'll remove his head and shit down the stump of his neck."

I handed him the bundle of hardware and turned to Jessie. "Go ahead. Tell him just what I told you."

Jessie spoke to her brother at length. When she was done, he gestured at me and asked her a question. Jessie blushed beet red and stammered out a one-word answer. Her brother looked at me with a new respect. He bowed slightly and smiled. "Ok, What did he ask?" I wanted to know."

Jessie blushed again. "He asked why you would protect me so fiercely." She said.

"And what did you tell him?"

She blushed even more. "He wanted to know if we were lovers." She hesitated again. "I said you were my betrothed."

I threw back my head and laughed. "Well why the hell not!" And I pulled her to me with my left arm and kissed her soundly.

Her brother watched all this with great amusement. Then he began examining the stuff taken from the mercenaries.
He asked Jessie a question, then looked at me. "He wants to know how you managed to kill the mercenaries." Jessie translated for me. "He wants to know where the rest of your men are."

"Tell him how it went down." I told her.

Jessie turned to her brother and they chattered back and forth for a while. Jessie looked back at me. "He wants to know how you killed all of them by yourself."

"There were only six of them." I said. "And I caught them off balance and never let them get set again."

Jessie translated for her brother. He laughed and clapped me on the shoulder. "He likes you." Jessie told me.

Jessie took my hand and led me to a large suite of rooms on the south wing of the house. "These are our rooms." She said.

"Can I get the bike brought inside? Someplace well ventilated and lit where I can work on it?"

"Of course." Jessie said. "I'll have it taken to the inner courtyard by the stables."

"Do your people understand distillation?" I asked Jessie.

She nodded. "We make grain alcohol for medicines and other purposes. Why?"

"Because I'll need pure alcohol to run my bike on when the gasoline runs out."

"I can get you a few barrels of pure alcohol." Jessie said. "But for right now, we have some unfinished business."

When I looked over at her, She was by the bed and was pulling her makeshift dress off over her head.

The last time I had passed up a chance to get a piece, she fanged my neck. I may be slow sometimes, but I seldom make the same mistake twice.

I shed my clothing as quickly as possible and joined Jessie on the bed. "Before we get started, just how old are you? The last thing I need is a statutory rape charge."

"I'm 40." Jessie said as she snuggled closer under the blankets.

"You're 40 years old? You don't look it." I said.

Jessie chuckled as she trailed kisses down my belly. "Not years silly, 40 decades." Then her mouth was too full to talk any more, and I was too distracted to continue the conversation. Well, except for things like, "Watch those damn teeth," etc.

Jessie was definitely not a novice at this, and I think I acquitted myself well, bringing her to climax at least three times.

I was so tired though, that I fell asleep with Jessie wrapped in my arms.

It was still light out when I went to sleep, but it was mid morning when I woke again. Sure enough, my neck ached again, and I found small scabs covering another set of fang marks.

Oh well, for sex like the last night, she could bite me now and then if she wanted.

The beautiful woman came silently into the room and gathered up the discarded clothing. "Ring when you want breakfast." she said softly when she saw that I was awake.

I looked over at Jessie, who was still sound asleep. " Breakfast can wait. Where is the garderobe?"

Garderobe? And I could understand her!

I fingered the punctures on my neck again. Unfinished business. Right.

The woman drew aside a curtain to reveal a door. "Right through here." She said.

Jessie pulled the covers over her head.

The woman smiled fondly at her and then left as silently as she had come. I got out of bed and opened the door behind the curtain. I could recognize a toilet with a tank atop a pipe over the toilet, and a dangling chain to flush it. There were soft corncobs to wipe with. I shrugged and just used the toilet. I felt much better after I was done. My morning breath would have to wait until I got at my duffle bag.

When I went back into the bedroom, I saw that my duffle was in the corner, as were my saddlebags.

I got out my toothbrush and the container that held the baking soda and salt mixture that I brushed with. I took care of that, then went back over to the bed.

I slipped under the covers and up to Jessie's back. I put my arm over her and she snuggled her backside more firmly against me. Well, I wasn't about to pass up an opportunity like this. And I was definitely rising to the occasion. Jessie woke up in the middle of some rather energetic sex, and picked up the pace considerably. When we were finished, Jessie scrambled out of the bed and trotted over to the bathroom.

I went and got out my old jeans and shirts, but couldn't bring myself to put them on. I piled them all on a chair, then sat down on the bed. Jessie came out of the toilet looking entirely too chipper.

"How do I go about getting this stuff washed?"

Jessie pulled on a tasseled rope hanging near the wall. A cute girl in a mini-dress came in a moment later. "Yes mistress?" She said to Jessie.

Jessie pointed at the pile of clothes on the floor. "Take these and have them cleaned. Have a tailor come to the house to outfit Bill here with clothing suitable to his station."

The maid nodded and gathered up the clothes. As she closed the door behind her, I looked up at Jessie. "And what is my station?"

Jessie came and sat next to me on the bed. She placed her hand on my thigh and squeezed. "As my fiancée, you have status equal to a minor lord." She said. "Above that, you are a warrior, and I think, we will also call you a sorcerer."

"Great." And what does that mean in terms I can understand?"

"Your social rank will be slightly above my brother's. And roughly equal to my father."

"Where does your father's rank stand at court? How does he compare to the ruler here?" I wanted to know.

Jessie thought it over. "Picture a staircase." she said. "If the king is the top step, our father is the next step down."

I had to think about that one. "And how will your parents feel about all this?"

Jessie blinked. "We are about to find out. The maid who answered the bell serves my mother.

Now the part I have always dreaded in any relationship since I was a teen was meeting the parents of my girlfriend. For some reason, this had never once gone real well. "I thought your parents were gone away to your other home."

Jessie smiled happily. "My brother must have sent word that I was back and with a prospective husband in tow."

"Right. Couldn't let a thing like that go by without telling the folks." I said dryly.

Jessie covered her mouth with her hands and giggled. "I wonder what he told them." She said.

I walked over to my saddlebags and dug out the cleaning kit for the .44 mag. I sat at a small table and started to clean the pistol. "Hey sweetheart, not that I mind being naked... but I really want to have some clothes on when I meet your folks. If your mother is as beautiful as you, I'd be standing there with a hard-on you could do chin-ups on."

Jessie agreed that might not make a good first impression. She slipped into a dress and went to go find out where my clothes were.

I found a bowl of fruit on a table close to the other side of the bed. I took an orange and some grapes and took them back to munch on as I finished cleaning the gun. When the .44 was clean and oiled, I put the cleaning kit away and broke out my sharpening kit for the Bowie. I love a sharp edge on a knife, and I had not touched the blade up as much as I should.

I put a razor edge on my knife, then coated the blade lightly with oil and slipped it back into place in my boot.

I used the toilet again, then used the water I found in a pitcher to wash up as best I could.

Jessie popped back in a half hour later by my watch. She had a pair of my black jeans, my wizard T-shirt, and socks and a pair of boxers. All was neatly cleaned and pressed. Even my Kevlar lined leather jacket was softer and cleaner than it had ever been.

I thanked her with a kiss and got dressed. I settled my gun belt on again, this time letting the gun ride at an angle in front of my left hip. I always favored a cross-draw whenever possible. Not as fast as a strong side draw, but easier to access when sitting down, and the gun is easily available to either hand.

I pulled my hair back into a ponytail at the nape of my neck, using one of my few remaining hair ties. I cleaned my glasses and I was ready to go. "So let's get this done." I told Jessie.

She smiled up at me and tucked her hand into the crook of my arm as we went out and down to where her parents awaited us.

I had a mental picture of good old Darth Vader in my minds eye, and I deliberately copied the confident stride and body language.

Head up and eyes straight, I entered the room with Jessie matching me step for step. The older man who looked to be about my age could only be her father. Her mother was so lovely that I would have been flying the flag if I weren't dressed.

We walked up to the couple. I bowed to Jessie's mother and looked her father in the eyes and held my hand out for him to shake. He met my gaze calmly, then shook my hand with a firm, confident grip.

"I am Ranal." He said in a vibrant baritone. "This is my wife, Cassandra." Jessie's mother nodded at me, he eyes friendly.

"I am Bill." I said. "It was my pleasure to aid your daughter when she was in need. And it is my great honor that she has chosen me for a husband."

"A warrior and a wizard my daughter tells us." Said Cassandra in a voice that put me in mind of angels.

"Marcus says that you are very protective of our daughter, to the point of threatening to remove his head and use his neck as a toilet." Ranal said conversationally.
"He was going to strike her." I said. "Jessie is a treasure to be cherished, not abused."

"Well said." came a voice from behind me. I turned slightly to see Marcus approaching. "Indeed, he came bearing the arms of 6 mercenaries that he slew single handed to save my dear sister." Marcus continued as he joined us.

Ranal visibly re-assessed me. "I would like to hear more about that fight." he said. Jessie tugged on her mother's sleeve. "Mother, at the altar of the Goddess in the circle stones, he placed coins, meat, blood and salt upon the altar. And the goddess spoke to me!"

Cassandra looked at her daughter with her eyes wide. "And what did the Goddess tell you?" "That Bill was to be my protector, my lover, and my mate." Jessie said. "She forbade me to ever lie to him or to disobey him. She said that our destinies are linked, and that he was brought here as a world walker to bring order and change." Ranal placed his hand on his daughter's head and closed his eyes. A moment later, she opened her mouth and spoke. "The time of war is upon us. A time when one man may save a world or drag it to ruin. One shall stand beside him, another at his back, the triad will be complete within the week, by then, the world walkers purpose will be known."

Jessie's eyes opened wide and rolled back up in her head. I caught her as she fell. Ranal leapt to pull a chair over for me to put her in. Cassandra sped off to fetch water.

Marcus looked at us in something like awe. "Well I'll be damned." he said.

Jessie revived quickly. She opened her eyes and threw herself into my arms, crying. I held her and stroked her hair and back.

I looked up at Ranal with a crooked smile. "Pre-wedding jitters?"

Ranal stared at me, then gave a great shout of laughter. " I think I like you after all." he said.

When Jessie was calmed down, I took her back up to our rooms and had her lay down. The tailor showed up and measured me carefully. He promised at least 3 sets of clothing by the end of the week. I thanked him and gave him a small gold bar from the stash I still had left.

"Tomorrow, I want to see the city." I told Jessie. "There is too much I don't know that I need to know. And you are the only one I trust to tell me and to keep me from making a fool of myself."
At supper that night, I managed not to embarrass myself too badly by imitating Ranal. He noticed this and gave me a small smile of approval.

Jessie kept the family entertained with a running account of my arrival, my fight, and the rest of the journey home.

When she repeated what I had told the innkeeper, Ranal laughed aloud. "I know the old miser." Ranal said. "And I doubt he'll be turning away any more of the Free Folk who pass his way."

"I need to find out where the rest of those roving mercenaries are." I said to Marcus. "I plan to rid the realm of them once and for all."

Marcus looked dubious. "There are far to many mercenaries to defeat all by yourself." He said. "Who said anything about doing all by myself?" I asked. "But to form an intelligent plan, I need to know how many, where they are, and how they are armed and equipped."

"The key to defeating an enemy with a large numerical superiority is being smarter and more mobile than he is." Ranal said.

"Exactly," I agreed. "Hit and run. Strike when least expected. Inflict maximum casualties, then fade away before the enemy can organize a counter-attack. Change tactics each time. Keep them paranoid and off balance."

It sounds like you have fought like this before." Said Marcus.

"Not me," I said. "My father fought an enemy called the Viet Cong in a far away land. They used these tactics and raised hell against the most powerful army on earth. Fought them to a standstill for a decade," I took a sip of wine. "Before that, the Na Dene and the Lakota among others did much the same. Eventually, the military of my land trained elite fighting men. Special forces who could go in small units and inflict casualties and damage that would take a normal army a hundred times as many men to accomplish."

Ranal sat back and looked at me with narrowed eyes. "Assuming that we could raise and train such a force. The equipment you carry and that vehicle you ride are beyond our means to duplicate in any reasonable amount of time."

"According to what Jessie said earlier. My being here is not an accident. That means that someone drew me here. If they can bring me across worlds, then they can send me back. I can easily bring back the weapons and supplies needed to equip a small force. We won't have time to train people to ride motorcycles, so horses will have to do. They're quieter anyway. Jessie can come with me to help me and to watch my back. I'm not real popular back home."

Cassandra spoke up then. "Will you not want to stay home there in your own place? This is not your home."

I reached over and grasped Jessie's hand. "It is now."

"Suppose the mercenaries are not the enemy the Goddess spoke of?" Ranal said thoughtfully. "Then they will make good practice for our forces to hone their skills on." I replied.

Ranal pushed back from the table. "I must talk to the king about this." He kissed his wife, bowed to the rest of us, and left.

Jessie looked up at her mother. "How soon can we be wed?"

"Tomorrow." Said Cassandra. She stood up and shooed Jessie and Marcus out of the room. "My future son in law and I need to talk."

Cassandra led me to a smaller room where we could talk without interruption. "You doubtless know by now that we are not wholly human." Cassandra began, "we are a long lived people. And rarely do we intermarry with full humans such as yourself." "I had that much figured out when Jessie bit me." I replied.

Cassandra smiled. "A useful mutation that we chose to breed for millennia ago."

"About Jessie's dowry," Cassandra started.

I held up my hand to stop her. "I will make my own way in this world as I did in mine. I do not ask for a dowry, nor would I accept one for her. To me, Jessie is enough in and of herself. Jessie can accept the dowry in her own name, to be used after I am gone. Jessie will long outlive me, and she should have something saved to fall back on after I have passed."

Cassandra looked at me solemnly. "I see that you do not fully understand. When my daughter chose you for a mate, she bound herself to you body, mind and soul. She will live a normal human life span. No more."

"I see." I said slowly. "This explains a lot."

Cassandra shook herself slightly and stood up. I rose to my feet and she took a step forward and embraced me. "I would not have chosen this path for her. But it was never my decision to make."
We went back to join the others. Jessie was practically dancing in her excitement. "Father bids you to come to the court!" she exclaimed. "And I am to accompany you."

I looked over to Marcus. "Will you come along?" I asked, "Things just might get interesting." He nodded with a small smile. "I foresee many interesting times ahead with you around."

Jessie tucked her hand into the crook of my arm. Marcus offered his arm to his mother, which she graciously accepted. Marcus and Cassandra led the way down to the courtyard where a carriage waited.

I leaned down close to Jessie's ear. "Well, it's no Harley, but I suppose it'll do this once."

I whispered. Jessie had to smother a fit of giggles at that. I waited for Cassandra to be seated, then I helped Jessie in.

I settled myself next to Marcus on the bench facing the ladies. "Enjoy the pleasures that come your way." I said to Marcus. "Such beauty as is before us happens only rarely in a mans life, even one as long as yours. Treasure these moments as if they were your last."

Marcus chuckled. "A warrior, a wizard, and now a gallant gentleman. I suppose you're a poet as well.'"

"The only verses that I know, are those unfit for mixed company, and those reserved for a man and his love."

Marcus lifted an eyebrow. "You'll have to teach me some of those verses." "Which sort?" I asked.

"Why, both of course!" He laughed outright, and the rest of us joined in.

"Do not be surprised by anything or anyone you see tonight. Not everyone who attends court is human, or even as close to human as we are." Cassandra said. "You are new and unknown, so you will be under more than usual scrutiny. Remember, do not take offense easily. There are those who like to test someone's temper just for fun."

"Don't worry," I said. "I'll behave myself. As long as no one offers to hurt or insult Jessie."

"And if someone insults me?" Cassandra's tone was cool and amused. "What will you do then?"

"Enjoy the spectacle of Marcus and your husband turning them into greasy smears on the floor." I said. "I doubt they would need my help. And if they did, I would give it." Jessie smiled proudly at me. At the palace, Marcus and I escorted the ladies inside. A page announced us as we entered the great hall. Cassandra was correct, there were creatures here that I couldn't have imagined in my worst nightmares. Nightmares, now there's an idea to store away for later.

Ranal appeared from the crowd and hurried towards us. "Come." he commanded. "The King and his consort wish to meet you."

He led us up to the thrones set on a dais at the far end of the room. The crowd melted away on either side like water parting around the bow of a ship. We halted a few steps from the dais.

The man on the throne looked like everyone's idea of a king. Tall, bearded, regal in his bearing. But there was something slightly off.

I glanced over at the man standing beside and slightly behind the throne. A plain looking man with sandy hair and a beak of a nose. Yet, he had more of an aura of command in his stance and body language.

I nodded to the man behind the throne. "Greetings Your Majesty."

Ranal clapped the man on the shoulder. "I told you that he wouldn't be fooled." The king came forward and took his place on the throne. The other man handed the king the crown and left the dais.

"Approach." The king said. I took a couple of steps forward and went to one knee.

"I am here to offer you my services, my loyalty, and my respect." I said.

I hadn't read all those books and watched all those movies for nothing ya know.

"Ranal has told me of your plans and your purpose here." The king said genially. "I am minded to give you rein to do as you must."

I was about to respond when I caught a movement out of the corner of my eye. The shield of the soldier standing where the king had just been was polished to a mirror finish. I could clearly see a man with a crossbow on a balcony above and to the side. He was aiming at someone on or near the dais.
I surged to my feet, shoving Jessie into her mother, and both of them went sprawling. I completed my turn, putting myself between the king and the crossbow man. I had begun drawing my .44 as soon as I had started moving, I brought it up into a two handed grip and fired as soon as the front sight covered the man.

3 times I pulled the trigger, riding the recoil and coming back down on target after each shot. Not shooting range accuracy, but the would be assassin was only about 40 feet away, and at that distance, no way I was going to miss.

The effect of the muzzle blasts from the .44 was astounding. Half the crowd hit the floor, and the other half headed toward the throne. They stopped fast enough when I pointed the gun at them. "Until I know friend from foe, stay where you are!" I bellowed.

Ranal had tackled the King and his consort off their thrones, and the one bolt the crossbow wielder got off was stuck in the wall above and behind the king's throne.

Marcus was suddenly by me side with a bared sword. I took the chance to reload the .44. If any more trouble erupted, I wanted a full cylinder. Jessie and her mother scurried over to where Ranal was helping the king to his feet.
Ranal stepped forward to the edge of the dais. "The audience is ended for tonight. Leave us."

Most of the crowd left peacefully enough except for one youthful looking woman who was giving the group around the throne some really poisonous looks. "Marcus, the lady in the blue and orange dress next to the crimson shield. Find some way to question her. I think that she may know something about this mess."

Marcus nodded and went over to whisper into a soldier's ear. The soldier glanced at me, then at the woman. He nodded once and disappeared through a side door.

"Ranal tells me that you are called Bill," said the king from behind me. I turned to face him and holstered the gun.

"He is correct, your majesty." I replied.

"After tonight, you may call me by my name as Ranal does." said the king. "I owe my life to you."

"I would be proud to call you by name, save that I have never heard it." I said with a smile. "And as for saving your life. Are you certain that it was you the assassin was aiming at? And how did he get through your guards with that big honking crossbow anyway?"

"Good questions both." frown the king. He turned to Ranal. "Find me the answers my old friend."

Ranal bowed slightly and left, calling out orders to the guards. "Jules." said the king. "Beg pardon?" I said, confused. "My name is Jules." the king clarified. "What is that thing that made such a noise?"

I took out the revolver and emptied it. I handed it to the king and explained how it worked. I showed him the cartridges and explained the reasoning behind the hollow points. The king was very bright and caught on at once. He asked intelligent questions for a good while. "Jules, could we move this to a more comfortable room, we have kept the ladies standing idly for far too long." I suggested.

"Quite right," said the king, "This way." And he led us to a small but comfortable room just behind the great hall.

Once the ladies were seated and the wine was poured, the king went on with his questions. A couple of hours later, Ranal joined us. "The assassin in the hall was dead when we got to him. We captured 3 others alive. One talked."
Ranal looked at me. "The assassin that you killed had holes in him as big as a fist, and most of his head was shattered."

The king looked at the .44 again with a new respect. "And you plan to bring more of those 'guns' to equip an elite force?"

"That is my plan." I said.

"Can you bring enough back to equip my palace guards?" asked the king.

"Easily." I replied.

“So be it.” Said the King. Turning his head to Ranal, he continued, “A fine addition to your family.”

We went home that night escorted by a contingent of the king's household guards. A squad of soldiers posted themselves in the outer courtyard as we entered the house.

Ranal and Cassandra said their good nights and retired to their rooms. Marcus, Jessie, and I went to Marcus' room to talk a bit more and to unwind with some fortified wine.

"By Hell, that toy of yours sounds like thunder and near made me unman myself." Marcus said. "And yet you say it is not the most powerful of its type?"

I sat back with a smile. Here I was on familiar ground. "We have easily carried guns that can reliably kill at distances of a thousand paces or more. And weapons so big they require vehicles or even ships to carry them that can shoot further than the eye can see and destroy a building such as this with one or two shots." I shook my head sadly. "And, I am sorry to say, we have other weapons that will destroy an entire city at once, and leave the ruins so poisoned that no living thing can enter them unharmed for 50 millennia."

Jessie looked frightened. "Your world must be a terrible place."

"There is beauty and art there as well." I said. "And the worst weapons, we dare not use, lest they be used against us."

"Madness!" said Marcus.

"You'll hear no argument from me about that." I drained my glass. "That is why I chose to make your struggles mine, and to remain here, where by some incredible fluke, a treasure such as Jessie could fall in love with a man like me."

Jessie rose from her seat and settled down in my lap. I smiled at Marcus. "Don't you think such a treasure is worth giving up a world for?"

Marcus snorted. "Hardly, but then, she's my baby sister."

Jessie poked her tongue out at Marcus, who laughed aloud. I picked up Jessie and headed for the door. "I shall see you tomorrow." I said to Marcus as we left.

"At the wedding." Marcus called after us.

The following day, Jessie was gone when I woke up. A new set of clothing was laid out for me. Black trousers and a silk tunic with the wizard and bikers picture embroidered on the front. I washed up and got dressed. I settled the gun belt on my hips again, and tucked my knife into my boot. There was a cloak made of the softest and lightest black leather I had ever seen. When I looked closely at it, I could see tiny scales giving it an almost iridescent sheen. I swung the cloak over my shoulders and fastened it with the pins provided. I looked in the full-length mirror. "Not bad at all." I mused aloud.

"I agree." said Ranal from the doorway. He came over to me and adjusted the cloak slightly. "The woman you pointed out last night was taken and questioned. She was only involved in the attempt on the king's life. However others she talked about while under the compulsion have proved elusive. The few we have found, indicate that someone has been summoning mercenary bands from all the known lands. For what purpose, we do not yet know. But it cannot be good for us."

I went over to the saddlebags and dug out couple of small boxes and took them to the desk. Ranal came over when I beckoned to him. I laid out the boxes and opened them. I took out a small chrome derringer and opened the action. I took a couple of cartridges and loaded both barrels. "This is a smaller, less powerful gun." I told Ranal. "It only fires two times before reloading, hut each cartridge holds 3 small balls which spread slightly after firing, thus increasing your chances of a hit." I worked the action a few times, then emptied the derringer and handed it to Ranal. "Practice loaded and reloading the derringer. Use it to protect yourself, Cassandra, and Jules."

Ranal hefted the derringer in his palm and stared at it grimly. "Such a small thing to be so deadly." He roused himself and tucked the derringer into his tunic. I handed him the box of ammunition. "Keep this hands, and find someplace private to practice. You now have a nasty surprise for any would-be assassins."

Ranal tucked the ammo box away. "Come, your wedding awaits."

I paused just outside the main hall and checked the loads in the .44.

"You expect trouble?" Ranal asked.

"No," I replied, "But I'm not about to take chances after last night."

Ranal nodded and checked the loads in the derringer.

I opened the big doors and strode into the room, followed closely by Ranal. The wedding was unlike any I had ever heard of. But nothing I couldn't deal with. I had the strangest feeling that there was someone watching us that I couldn't see. Jessie and her mother kept casting nervous glances at the shrine of the Goddess set in the wall not far from the dais where we all now stood. I answered the questions the priestess asked, and followed instructions as best I could under the circumstances. I found myself wishing that someone had thought to rehearse me at least once. But I managed to muddle through OK. No trouble materialized during the wedding or the banquet that followed. Any of the guests that would have entertained ideas about testing the newcomer had either witnessed, or heard of, the incident at the Royal court the previous evening.
Jules attended of course, as did his consort Larilea. His son Prince Jalan was there also, but he was not entirely thrilled about the wedding. I suspected that he had entertained plans for Jessie himself. Too bad. He should have moved faster.

Jessie was radiant in a cream colored silk dress that I was willing to bet had cost more than my first two houses combined. Dancing was slow and easy to follow, although the music was a little odd to my ears. But then, I figured that they would think much the same about Ozzy.

When all the fuss was done and over with, I spirited Jessie upstairs to our rooms and locked the door, wedging a chair inter the latch to make double sure.

It took longer than I liked to get than damned dress off my bride, but we managed finally to get rid of our encumbrances and tumble onto the bed. Jessie responded to my love making with a passion that was astonishing, and she had never been exactly quiet or passive during sex before Once, someone pounded on the door and shouted at us to come join the party, but we ignored them, being quite happy where we were.

The next morning, Jessie and I went out walking to the marketplace. I watched and listened and learned. Jessie was a big help as I had expected. But it was the conversations that I over heard proved to be the most enlightening. I drew some stares, but as with any big city, the unusual was the rule rather than the exception, so I was not overly conspicuous.

After all, seeing a man in a black cloak walking with a lovely girl is hardly interesting when your last customer resembled a tarantula the size of a Clydesdale horse!

All told, an interesting and educational day. Jessie and I ate at an outdoor cafe that served an excellent stew and fresh hot bread. Jessie was excited and proudly displayed the bracelets and necklace that proclaimed her to be a married woman. I kept my eyes and ears open as we did our shopping.

I made a deal with a distillery to deliver several barrels of pure grain alcohol to the house. Then I stopped by an alchemist's shop and bought a few useful items. Carrying our purchases, Jessie and I started home.

I noticed that someone was following us. "Jessie, when I give the word, turn into the next alley, take 5 steps and press yourself against the wall."

Jessie reached behind her and drew a needle sharp dagger, holding it in the folds of her cloak.

I gave her a nudge, and we wheeled sharply into the alley, Jessie pressed her back into a doorway, and I flattened my back against the wall. A few seconds later, A man came running around the corner. I grabbed his arm and slammed him against the wall. I snatched his sword and dagger from their sheathes and tossed them to the ground at Jessie's feet. I drew the .44 and pressed it up under the man's chin. "You'd better have a really good reason for following us." I said.

I heard a sound behind me, a blade coming out of the sheath. I pressed the trigger of the .44 and spun to the side and away to face the newcomer.

I saw an unfamiliar face, and a bare blade. That was enough for me. I shot him.

A third man turned to run, but Jessie’s dagger flashed past me to bury its blade in the man's thigh. I strode forward as he staggered and sledged him across the back of the head with the butt of the .44 before he could regain his feet. "Good thinking," I told Jessie as she yanked her blade from the man's leg and wiped it on his cloak. "We can question this one."

Jessie looked sheepish. "I was aiming at his heart and missed." she admitted as she sheathed her dagger.

We waited where we were, sure enough, City guards were drawn to the sound of the fight. The recognized Jessie, and they had heard tales of the assassination attempt at the palace. Now they got to see first hand the results of close range .44 magnum rounds. The first man's head was mostly gone from the eyes up, and the other had a nice hole punched through the steel breastplate he was wearing under his tunic.

The guards picked up the bodies and the unconscious man and carried them all to Jessie's house.

Jessie was still running on an adrenaline high, but she told her story clearly, and omitted no major details. I didn't have much to add at that point. Ranal dismissed the guards with a nice bonus for each.

Ranal sent a maid to fetch Marcus. "We need to get this man to a healer, and then we need to question him." He told his son. Marcus just slung the man over his shoulder and carried him out to the family carriage.

Ranal followed him out. I took Jessie up to our rooms and sent a maid for Cassandra.
Cassandra and Jessie started talking and I went down to the stables to get to work on the Harley. I adjusted the carburetors to allow for a gasoline, alcohol mix. I hoped I could find some way to get more oil, or that would end the engine as surely as lack of gas.

When I had the tank full of the fuel mixture, I started the bike and rode it around the courtyard once. Then parked it.

Back inside, I had the maid's fill a large tub with warm water and I took a much-needed bath. When I was done, I had the butler take me to the library room and bring me a pen, paper and ink. I made a list of the things I wanted to bring back with me. A handbook on basic chemistry, more ammo for the derringer and the .44. Medicines, spices and seasonings, a tool kit. A book on petroleum distillation. And books on tactics and strategy. I thought about it, then added a CD player and some CD's, and a solar power battery charger and rechargeable batteries. I sat back and thought for a while. I knew where I could get a bunch of AK47's and SKS rifles and more than enough ammo. Pistols, probably the Chinese copies of the Tokarev in 9mm, and the copy of the Colt 1911A1 .45 auto. I could probably scare up some shotguns and ammo. Reloading presses and powder, primers and bullets. Empty brass wouldn't be a problem. Hell, if I shopped around, I could probably get some hand grenades, LAWS rockets and RPG7's. Radios and binoculars, scopes and deer rifles that would make excellent sniper weapons.

I remembered the thought about giving the enemy nightmares and added a few thousand doses of LSD and other hallucinogens to the list. A couple of military surplus trucks to haul all this shit back with me. And while I was at it, How about a couple of m-60's and M2 machine guns.

When I was done with the list hours later, I blew on the ink to dry it, then capped the inkwell and went up to my rooms.

Jessie was asleep in bed already. So I undressed as quietly as I could and snuggled up to her back. She murmured in her sleep and pushed her butt back against me. I slid my arm around her and cupped her breast with my palm.

I was asleep in seconds. My sleep was haunted by nightmares and strange dreams. I woke up the next morning still tired, and in a cranky mood. Jessie cured me of the mood right away though. She pulled me over atop her for a good morning quickie.

Feeling much better, we ate breakfast with the others. I showed Ranal the list, and explained that I was going to need 2 people and about a hundred pounds of gold to get it all and get it back home. "Jessie goes with me." I said. "That's a given, and I can teach her to drive well enough, but I'll need someone else I can trust. Someone who won't panic at strange things and stranger ideas."

Ranal looked at his son. "Marcus, you will go with them. Consider yourself under Bill's orders until you return with whatever this 'stuff' is."

Marcus grinned like a shit eating dog. "This sounds like fun."

"There will be fun." I told him. "But we will have to travel unarmed for most of the time, and a wrong word or gesture can get us all killed."

Marcus sobered abruptly. "Of course." he said contritely.

"Now how are we supposed to travel back to my world?" I asked.

Cassandra spoke up. "At the stone circle where you made the offering, you will spend the night. In the morning, when you emerge from the mist, you will be back home. When you are ready to return, your wife will use her icon to summon the Goddess' aid."

I took a deep breath. "I'll need at least 2 of your most skilled smiths." I told Ranal. “And a master cabinetmaker. Once they have finished with what I need, we can leave."

"They will be here this morning." Ranal promised.

Most of the rest of the day was spent in designing a sidecar for the Harley to hold Marcus and the gold.

By the third day, the sidecar was finished and tested. I put on my old biker clothes and had Jessie and Marcus dress similarly.

We said our goodbyes and loaded the Harley into an enclosed wagon to be taken well outside of the city and the canyon gates.

Out of sight of prying eyes, we unloaded the bike and sent the wagon on its way to pick up supplies from a nearby town.

Marcus rode in the sidecar with the gold, Jessie rode behind me, holding me tightly around the waist and pressing her cheek into my back.

After we left the vicinity of the towns, the only things we saw were a flock of sheep and something very large flying off in the distance. If it wasn't a dragon, it was the first cousin to one, and I was glad of the distance between us.
We reached the stone circle without incident. I drove right between the upright stones and parked next to the altar. I placed gold, meat and salt, and each of us offered a few drops of blood. A mist had gathered as soon as we had entered the circle, and now it enclosed the shrine entirely. In the morning, we mounted up and I drove carefully through the mist. Half seen shapes loomed in the mist and were gone, then abruptly,

the mist was gone. I braked to a stop and looked around to get my bearings.

Marcus was pale, but calm. Jessie was trembling against my back like she was in an earthquake. I had huge butterflies in the pit of my stomach, but they were easing fast.

I spotted familiar landmarks. We were in Arizona, about 10 miles from the border. I stowed the .44 in the sidecar and we jounced along until we reached a road. That road took us to a paved highway. Marcus was shaking now at the sight of all those cars and trucks etc. whizzing by. Jessie just clung tighter to me and kept her face buried against my back.

I headed for Nogales. A smooth and easy trip by then, and Marcus and Jessie settled down a lot.

But that iron-shod wooden wheel for the sidecar was in sorry shape by the time we hit Nogales proper, and the noise it made on the pavement was maddening after a while.
We were waved through the border without comment, although I saw the US Customs people making notes of my license number.

I stopped at a little bodega and bought a few switchblade knives just in case. Then we rode out to old Don Tomas de la Torres place.

The old reprobate was thrilled to see me, and he made much of Jessie and Marcus. I explained to him that Jessie spoke only English, and Marcus did not even speak English or Spanish.

I showed Don Tomas the list I had made up. "Don Tomas, I know that a man of your wisdom and power can help me to find these things that I desperately need."

Don Tomas studied the list. "I can do this thing, but my friend, the cost. I am afraid it will be very high."

I handed Don Tomas one of the gold bars that Marcus had carried from the sidecar. "A hundred pounds of this should more than pay for what we need."

Don Tomas' eyes lit up as he saw the buttery gleam of the gold. "If this is oro, as it appears, then yes, that should be enough and more."
He had his niece Maria take us to a suite of rooms in one wing of the mansion.

"Don Tomas came to us a few hours later. "All is being gathered and will be ready in two days." he said.

I sent Marcus down to the motorcycle to bring up the remaining gold bars. When he came back with the boxes of gold, Don Tomas was astounded. "You brought it all with you?" He asked.

"Don Tomas," I replied. "We are both men of honor. I knew that you would never cheat me, as I would never cheat you."

Don Tomas called for one of his bodyguards to carry the gold away. When we were alone, he sat down and picked up the phone. He spoke rapid fire Spanish far to quickly for me to follow. Then he hung up. "I had the supplier add a little bonus to your order." he said. The old man stood up and embraced me, pounding my back with his hands. "Honor is so rare these days." he said. "If more young men were like you, I would need no bodyguards."

I had long been out of pipe tobacco, and when I mentioned this, Don Tomas gave me a dozen pounds of his private blend, and a case of fine Cuban cigars.

Jessie he gave a beautiful dress and a set of pearl earrings.

Marcus, he gave a dagger that had been in his family for generations.

Jessie kissed the old man on the cheek. "Our first born son will carry your name." she said to him.

Marcus found plenty of company among Don Tomas' maids. They found his looks irresistible.

By the time we left, Marcus had acquired a working vocabulary in both Spanish and English. He was careful to conceal this knowledge however. As he put it one evening, "No sense in giving away an advantage."

Don Tomas had his people teach Marcus and Jessie to handle the big 2 1/2 ton trucks that would carry all of our gear. Finally, the trucks were loaded, and we were ready to leave. Don Tomas accompanied us to the gates of his hacienda. "Farewell my friends."

"Good bye Papa Tomas!" Called out Jessie as we pulled out. The old man stood there waving until we were out of sight.

We stopped for the night about 40 miles from Nogales on a dry lakebed. Jessie clutched her Icon and began chanting. The now familiar mist gathered. More slowly this time. When our watches said it was near dawn, we started up the trucks and moved out. I led the way, with Jessie about a foot off my rear bumper, and Marcus bringing up the rear.

When we broke out of the mist, we found ourselves in the middle of a sprawling military camp. There were lots of different banners. Too many for it to be anything but a mercenary camp. I floored the accelerator. The roar of the diesel motors behind me told me that Jessie and Marcus had the same idea. I aimed for the biggest tents around, figuring that if I could at least scare hell out of the leaders, they would be longer in arranging pursuit.

I tore through the tents at almost 50 miles per hour, rumbling over something I sincerely hoped were the mercenary leaders. We raced out of the camp and off across the plains as fast as we could push the trucks. Marcus actually passed me, grinning like a maniac and screaming something I couldn't hear over the noise of the engines.

We were a good 40 or 50 miles from the mercenary camp when Marcus slowed to a stop. I pulled up next to him and shut down the engine. Jessie pulled up on the other side of him and shut down her truck.

Marcus climbed down and trotted over to me. Jessie was already hugging me and laughing. Marcus hugged both of us. "Did you see them scatter?" Marcus shouted. "They must think all the demons of hell are after them!"

I heard something in the back of Marcus' truck. We went around to the back of the truck. Marcus untied the canvas flap and flipped it open. A tousled head popped up over the tailgate. "Who the hell taught you to drive, a damn monkey?" It was Don Tomas maid Consuela.

Marcus rolled his eyes. "Well isn't anyone going to help me down?" Consuela demanded.

Marcus stepped up and helped her to the ground. Consuela dusted herself off, cussing up a storm in Spanish and English. Then she looked up. Consuela let out a strangled scream and fainted dead away.

I spun and dropped my hand to my pistol. Jessie saw my movement and put a hand on my forearm to stop me. Marcus turned a lot more calmly, holding Consuela's limp form.

I was face to nose with a big winged beastie that looked an awful lot like a dragon. The dragon pulled its head back and sat up on its haunches. "Dear me," the dragon said. "I didn't mean to frighten anyone, I was just curious to see what was raising such a commotion way out here on our borders."

I looked at Jessie for advice. For once I was completely at a loss for words.

Jessie stepped forward. "I am Jesselle, wife of Bill, and daughter of Ranal, Councilor to King Jules." She placed her hand on my shoulder. "This is my husband, the Warrior-Wizard." She moved over to her brother. "This is Marcus, my brother. And Consuela our servant."

The dragon nodded to each of us. "I am called Skyfire in your tongue. I am on duty patrolling our borders. There has been much unrest of late, and there is a large army of mercenaries not far from here."

I stepped forward. "We are pleased to meet you Skyfire." I said. "We do not mean to trespass on your domain. Simply give us directions and we will be on our way."

The dragon chuckled and leaned down to rest it's chin on crossed forelegs. "We are not so unfriendly as that." said Skyfire. "You are most welcome to visit our realm any time you come in peace."

Consuela woke up and saw the dragon again. She promptly fainted again, this time without all the theatrics. "Does she always do that when she sees a dragon?" Skyfire asked curiously. "She has never seen a dragon." I said. "Dragons are known only as myth and legend in her world."

Skyfire reared back in surprise. "World-walkers!" "Remain here." Said the dragon. Giving a tremendous leap upwards, the dragon took flight and vanished into the distance.

I started setting up camp. "Come on folks. Looks like we stay here for the moment."

Marcus laid Consuela down and helped set up the tarp between two of the trucks. Jessie built a small fire and started cooking supper. While we were eating, Consuela woke up. She stared wildly around. "Diablos!" she screamed at us and ran off into the dark.

We searched but could not find her. Marcus stopped us from going far into the darkness. "There are too many beasts that hunt the night around here. They will not approach the fire or the trucks, but out there alone..." He shook his head.
The morning found entire squadrons of dragons spiraling down out of the sky to land around us. It was a beautiful and scary sight.

Skyfire landed next to us, followed by a dragon that could easily take one of the trucks in one bite.

"We saw the remains of your servant Consuela about 2 miles from here. It looks like a pack of wolves found her." Skyfire informed us.

"She panicked and ran off into the dark." I said.

Skyfire shook his head. "I hope she passed quickly. There was not much left."

The big dragon spoke then, "I am the seer for the dragon folk. Why do you walk between worlds?"

Jessie told the dragon of the first night at the shrine, and the Goddess transporting us between worlds to bring back what could save the world.

"Or destroy it." rumbled the big dragon. "Yes, I know the prophecy, and I too have been visited by the Goddess, even tough she is not one we worship ourselves."
I stood there in front of the big dragon, probably the bravest thing I had ever done considering that I wanted to find someplace nice and safe and hide for the next few millennia.

The old dragon regarded me silently for a long moment, then nodded. We shall help you." Some quick noises in what I took to be dragonese and the dragons all lifted off, circling once and flying off in the direction we had come from.

"Let's get packed and get out of here." I said. "Marcus, you know the land better than I do, you lead the way."

Marcus gestured at Jessie, "She knows the land around here far better than I do." He said. "I will lead if you want, but she is the better choice."

I looked at Jessie. "OK then sweetheart, you lead off, Marcus follows, and I will bring up the rear."

Jessie gave me a quick kiss, then we broke camp and headed out. Around dusk, we approached the first gate. It opened before we had a chance to stop. We continued on. The second gate was open when we got there. And the gates to the city were open and well it. It was a tight squeeze getting the trucks through the main street to the palace. We managed to get the trucks around into the inner courtyard without any major mishaps.
Jules himself came down to greet us. "A dragon flew in and told us that you were coming." He said. "Welcome back."

King Jules issued orders to have the trucks unloaded and the gear stored in the palace vaults. "Jules, I am sorry," I said. "But we are tired, and hungry and sore, can we visit and brief you tomorrow?"

Jules looked abashed. "Yes, yes, I should have thought of that. How careless of me." He patted each of us on the shoulder and told us to go home and rest.

I saw the Harley unloaded, so Marcus, Jessie and I climbed on, fired it up and rode home.

Ranal and Cassandra greeted us as we parked the bike by the stables. Cassandra called to the maids to bring food and wine to the main dining hall. Ranal and Cassandra had enough sense not to ask too many questions until we had eaten our fill.

As we relaxed with goblets of wine, Jessie and I brought them up to date about the success of the mission and the incident with the dragons. Marcus provided much needed details about the mercenary encampment. He claimed he had more time to notice details as he simply steered wherever my truck was going at the moment.

Marcus laughed at the recollection of a mercenary captain standing up with his mouth open just in time to get a face full of speeding truck.

Ranal congratulated him for his keen eye and keeping his wits about him. "The mission could not have succeeded without him." I said. Marcus preened visibly.

I couldn't resist. "And he made quite an impression among the young ladies of my world as well."

Marcus sobered quickly. "Too much of one it seems." He told Ranal and Cassandra about poor Consuela.

Ranal shook his head. "It was her own foolishness that got her killed." He declared. Cassandra nodded her agreement.

Finally, we excused ourselves and headed to bed. Jessie snuggled close with her arms tight around me and was sleeping within moments. I lay there a while, stroking her hair and back, then I closed my eyes and drifted off to sleep.

Ranal let us sleep to noon, then had his wife come wake us. "Marcus has already been summoned to the palace, now you must get up and get ready to join him."

Jessie stretched and yawned, showing her needle like fangs for a moment before they retracted. Cassandra saw my look and giggled. "You will get used to them in time." she said.

Jessie and I dressed and rushed through breakfast.

Then we rode the Harley to the palace courtyard. Jules and Marcus greeted us there. They had samples of the guns and ammunition laid out on tables in the shade of the stables. "Come and tell me how these things work." Jules said.

I had Marcus get the stable boys to fill bags with sand and stack them against the far wall. When they had a stack about 6 feet high, and 5 feet long and bout 3 feet thick, I picked up an AK47. "This is an assault rifle." I told the king. "It fires one of these." And I held up the 7.62x39 cartridge. "This particular gun holds 30 in this magazine." And I loaded the clip. "The magazine goes here like so," And I clicked the magazine into place. "You pull this back and let it go forward, this feeds the first round into the chamber." I demonstrated. "Then you flick the safety off." and I showed them how.

I explained how to use the sights. Then had them practice sighting with an empty gun. I had a kitchen worker hang a side of beef from a tripod in front of the sandbags.

"The gun can fire either one shot each time you pull the trigger." And I fired a pair of shots in semi auto mode. "Or you can empty the magazine in a single burst." And I flipped the selector to full auto and blew the side of beef into burger.

"Dear Goddess!" Jules said as he inspected the damage done to the beef.

Jules ordered the man that I had knocked out in the alley brought out and stood in front of the sandbags. He loaded the magazine on his AK without fumbling, showing that he had been paying close attention. He clicked the magazine into place and aimed at the man. His thumb moved the selector to full auto and he squeezed the trigger. Literally blown to pieces, the man collapsed in a spray of blood and tissue.

Jules regarded the rifle in his hands grimly. "I could almost wish that I had not introduced such a hellish weapon into the world."

I demonstrated the other guns that I had brought. The king particularly liked a Beretta 9mm that had been nickel-plated. I gave it to him along with a holster and a case of 9xl9mm hollow-point bullets. "Practice daily." I told him. "Go for smooth on the draw. Fast will come of it's own accord. But a lightning draw does no good if you miss your shot."

Marcus preferred to use my old .44. I gave it to him along with a case of ammunition.

Jessie and I had a matched set of Para-Ordinance P-16 .45 autos. 16+1 shots and we could interchange ammo and magazines.

I had to decline to demonstrate the RPG's and other heavy weapons right there, saying that they were far too dangerous to demonstrate in an enclosed area. "Then tomorrow, outside city walls." Jules said.

On that note, we took our leave, and a few toys, and went home.

Cassandra received a Ladysmith 9mm with a pink polymer grip. Ranal got a black Beretta 9mm just like the king's, so they could interchange ammo and clips. I also handed out Mexican switchblade knives to all for a last ditch surprise.

Cassandra had a few people over for supper that evening. The cooks had a ball with the spices and seasonings that I had brought back. Although I had to put up with a pair of bites on the neck so the head cooks could understand the cookbooks and the labels on the packaging.

The dinner party was a success, and Cassandra was at her radiant best.

Ranal was a gracious host, keeping everything going smoothly. Jessie, Marcus and I just enjoyed the food and the company.

After the dinner, some of the guests stayed over.

Jessie practically raped me as soon as we got into the bedroom.

When I woke up in the morning, we were not alone in the bed. A couple of the guests from last night had joined us during the night. They were a pair of young ladies that I had noticed during the dinner because of their remarkable similarity and the fact that they had short silky fur all over their bodies, cat like triangular ears set high on their heads, vertical slit pupils in their eyes, and yard long fuzzy tails.

They were tumbled over Jessie and me like boneless furry blankets, and they purred in their sleep.

Jessie woke up with a mouthful of fur and turned her head toward me. "Pah!" She spit out the hairs stuck in her mouth.

"Chenna and Varra." she said in exasperation. "I knew we should have locked that damn door."

"So that's why the bed seems crowded." I quipped. Jessie made a face and I gave her a firm kiss to start the day.

Jessie and I wriggled out of bed and started dressing. The cat girls kept right on sleeping. Jessie shook her head. "They're harmless." She said fondly. "They were my best friends while I was growing up."

"Looks like you will have someone to keep you busy today while I go take the King and crew out to start training." I said.

Jessie grinned. "We're all coming with you. I'm in this too, remember?"

She reached out and tweaked the tails of the sleeping girls. They woke up fast, yowling and hissing with all of their fur standing on end. They looked at Jessie and started wicked smiles.

My loving wife shook her head and pointed at me.

I got pounced from three sides at once.

I had never believed that there could be too much of a good thing until that morning. I was wrong. I am a lot stronger than I look, but in mere moments, I was thoroughly pinned to the floor by 3 giggling females. They were all a lot stronger than they looked too. When the ladies finally let me up, we were almost late for our meeting with the king. A hurried breakfast with Marcus, then out to the deuce and a half that Marcus had already brought around earlier.

Ranal and Cassandra rode up front with Marcus driving.

Chenna and Varra rode in back with Jessie and me. "What's all this stuff for?" One of the cat girls asked.

"We're going to war." Jessie told them.

"Too much noise and too much stink." said the other cat girl, wrinkling her nose in distaste. I agreed with them, but kept my thoughts to myself.

As best I could figure, Chenna was the one with the white spot on her right cheek, and Varra had the white spot on her left cheek. To test my theory, I said "Chenna, where do your folk come from?"

The girl with the spot on the right looked up. "Our people were created long ago by wizards who wanted a race of hunters and fighters. They blended humans, Free Folk, and various big cats. The ones who looked more like the cats had more of the cat minds as well. They rebelled and killed the wizards who created them. They live mostly in the forests and mountains west of the Dragon Peaks. Those of us who looked and acted more like humans and Free Folk came here to live. We are never numerous. But any human or free folk who breed with one of our kind produces only catkin. The mutation still breeds true."

"So you have the longevity of the Free Folk." I said.

Varra nodded, "we live very long lives compared to mortals, but we are also slow to mature, and breeding catkin to catkin is rarely successful."

"Mostly we are dancers, concubines, bodyguards, consorts, and soldiers." Chenna said. "The two of is are sisters from the same litter. When a catkin woman breeds with a human or Free Folk male, there is always a multiple birth. When a human or Free Folk woman breeds with a catkin man, the results are single births or twins."

"So how did you meet Jessie?" I asked.

Jessie blushed beet red. Varra gave a silvery laugh, "When Jessie was a mere 12 years old, a year younger than us, we caught her spying on our older brother as he made love to his Free Folk mistress."

"I was curious." Jessie protested weakly. "Jesselle had a crush on our brother." teased Chenna.

"And our brother knew she was spying on him. We have very good hearing you know." Varra said, she flicked an ear to emphasize the point. "So he deliberately put on a show that nearly exhausted his lover, and strained his back so he could barely walk for a week."

The catkin girls laughed and Jessie blushed, but finally joined the laughter.

The truck slowed, then turned off the road. We bounced around in the back of the truck for a few minutes, then the truck came to a stop. We heard the cab doors open, so I climbed down and turned to help the ladies down.

' I collected a kiss from Jessie as a toll for lifting her down.

Jules was waiting for us near a wagon piled with crates and boxes. He smiled warmly when he saw Jessie and the girls. "So the terrible triad is united again."

Jessie winced a bit, then grinned back. I wondered what mischief the three of them had been into in the past, but put the thought aside. I had more than enough else to worry about just now.

The king wanted me to demonstrate some of the heavier weapons for him. So I blew apart various trees and boulders with the RPG-7 and a LAWS rocket. Grenades were a big hit, with Chenna and Varra throwing them with amazing accuracy and range. The heavy and light machine guns chewed up the countryside rather well. But the flamethrowers were set aside as too inhumane.

Chenna and Varra wanted matching pistols. So we gave them a pair of the Para Ordnance P16 .45's complete with gun belts, clips, cleaning kit, and of course, ammo.

I set everyone down on the ground with cloths spread out in front of them. I led them through disassembling and cleaning their guns, then putting them back together.

Over and over I drilled them until they could take down their guns and put them back together blindfolded.

In the later afternoon, soldiers and anyone else who wanted to try out for the elite forces ran improvised obstacle courses, demonstrated hand to hand combat, and feats of strength, speed, and endurance. We weeded them down to the best hundred, and then to the best 50.

At the end of the day I went to the King. "Jules, I can make your elite forces from these men. Only 1 in 5 will graduate. But they will form the core to train others. Send to any who have mastered some form of combat and offer them top wages to train your troops."

"That will be very expensive." frowned Jules.

"How much is your kingdom worth?" I asked. Jules nodded, but he wasn't thrilled.

I told the finalists to meet me in the same place in the morning an hour after dawn.

Then everyone trooped back to town. I told Marcus to leave the truck at the palace in the morning and we would all ride out in a wagon like the troops.

Over the next few days, we weeded more out. Men who could not learn to shoot. Those who could not co-operate with others, and the stupid.

We ended up with a mixed force. Men and women, human, free folk, and catkin.

I taught what little martial arts I knew. A piss poor mix of Karate, Judo and aikido. But it was still better than the crude punches and kicks that constituted hand-to-hand combat in this world.

On the 5th day, a Sword-master showed up. He got the troops for 2 hours per day. I had instituted a regimen of calisthenics that I recalled from my old army days. I got into better shape along with the rest. I taught firearms and explosives along with basic tactics.

Another Master showed up. This one teaching a form of hand to hand that resembled karate. He took over a couple of hours per day as well.

We soon had squads organized who trained and lived and played together. A catkin man who had made an art form of night fighting was added to the roster.

We even had a crew of soldiers, mostly older retirees, who did nothing but reload our empty ammunition casings. A group of alchemists were put to work developing a substitute for the gunpowder and another group were set to work duplicating the primers. The books I brought back were a huge help, but I was getting tired of my neck feeling like a pincushion from all the damn bites so the alchemists could read the books.

Everything was going fine on the military front. Dragons were doing aerial recon for us, keeping tabs on the mercenaries' movements.

We were sometimes able to evacuate towns before the mercenaries got there. When we failed, they left no one alive but a few girls who were carried off and later raped to death. My troops were angry and itching to hit back.

On the home front however, things were not quite that smooth. Chenna and Varra had moved into our rooms with us. "We heard all about the attack in the alley." Varra said. "Where Jesselle goes, we go. Between us, no one will get to her."

While I had no problem with that, the catkin girls seemed to delight in walking in on my wife and me while we were busy screwing each other’s brains out. And of course, they slept in the bed with us. "We don't mind." Chenna said once when they walked in on us. "We've seen it all before."

Then the damn girls sat down to watch and offer critiques of my style. They were only kidding. I think. But it was damn distracting. Jessie found the whole situation too funny for words.

But I soon found the catkin's weakness. They're ticklish. ESPECIALLY their tails

Jessie and the twins would gang up on me when I got too big for my britches, and only a good tickling could save me from a similar fate. Since catkin don't need much in the way of clothing, being covered in that soft dense fur, most of the time Chenna and Varra wore only a short shift dress, or nothing at all when they were in our rooms and relaxed.

I designed a halter top for them and a pair of shorts, complete with a hole in the back for the tail. And all three girls took to wearing these outfits when they were at home.

Soon Cassandra had some made for her, and the sight of her in a halter and shorts made every man who saw her that way drooling. Marcus and me included. Ranal noted the looks and almost strutted as Cassandra so obviously doted on him.

Marcus was in charge of the troops once I had taught all I was capable of. I reserved my time for teaching tactics and strategy to the officers and non-coms. We had set up ranks based on armies in my world, mostly for my convenience, although I did not tell them that.

Even Jules' consort Larilea was wearing the new, comfortable clothing when securely in their private apartments. Before long, other women were copying the clothes, and a fad had started.

Marcus was friendly with Varra and Chenna, but his true affections were reserved for a raven-haired beauty named Lai. A shy girl whose family was related to Larilea's. She obviously adored Marcus, and he loved her whole-heartedly.

They were married 2 months after our return from my world. Lai became a regular visitor to our rooms when Marcus was away. She was lonely, and in a new home in a new city. Jessie and the catkin twins immediately adopted her as a kid sister.

For me, this meant a 4-way pounce instead of a 3 way pouncing. Lai lost her shyness once she got to know us, revealing a lively sense of humor and an incredibly sharp intellect. She remained shy around crowds and strangers, but among family, she was not above bawdy practical jokes and driving her husband to distraction.

I came home late one evening, tired and half asleep. I had long since designed a shower and had it installed in the bathroom. This night, I used the shower, dried off, the climbed naked into bed. I wondered dully where the catkin twins were, then slid under the covers and snuggled up to my wife.

It was a full 20 or 30 seconds before I figured out that the naked lady I was cuddled up to was NOT my wife. I sat up and threw the covers back. "What the fuck!?"

Lai sat up, bare as an egg. "Surprise!" she yelled. The lights flared up and Jessie, the twins, and Marcus came out from behind the drapes where they had been hiding and watching their prank unfold.

Lai got on her hands and knees to crawl off the end of the bed, laughing like hell. Her delectable butt was wagging in the air as she crawled past me. So I gave into temptation and bit it. Not hard, just a nip on the left cheek. Lai squawked and leaped halfway across the room, bringing another round of laughter.

Marcus helped his wife up and then sat down with her in his lap. I got pounced by Jessie and the twins, with everyone laughing and having a fine time.

From that night on, Lai would come to me for a hug and a kiss just like the others.

Marcus didn't mind at all. In fact, one night he gave me express permission to have his wife if I wanted. "I appreciate the offer my brother." I told him. "But your sister is enough to handle. Besides, in my world, making love to a friends wife is considered wrong."

"We're not in your world." Marcus pointed out. "And I want a bond to grow between you and Lai in case I am killed in the war."

"She will always have a place in my heart, and in my home." I answered Marcus. "I guess I still have to get over being a one woman man."

"You mean you're not even having sex with the twins?" Marcus demanded, shocked.

"No." I replied,

Marcus reached out and smacked me upside the head, hard. "I never figured you for a damn fool." my brother in law said. "Do you really think that Jessie would ALLOW other women into your bed if she didn't WANT and EXPECT you to love them?"

He shook his head, muttering something about damn-fools and someone needing a kick in the butt to get their brain started again.

"I get the idea. Sheesh." I said.

I went upstairs and found Jessie sitting at her table cleaning her gun. Lai and the twins were off somewhere plotting mischief. "Honey, your brother, a man I would kill and die for, tells me that I have been a damn fool."

Jessie planted her elbow on the table and propped her chin on her hand. "How so my love."

"Marcus tells me that you have been expecting and wanting me to make love to the twins." I said.

"Why else would I bring them to our bed?" Jessie asked.

"That's what Marcus said too." I replied. "He also wants me to be with Lai to build a bond in case something happens in the war."

Jessie nodded. "That would be a great idea for all of us." Jessie said. She saw my look and hurried on. "I have looked deep into your mind, my love. And I know this is foreign to you."

"That's for sure." I muttered.

Jessie ignored the interruption. "You are a good man. And I trust you and our love to last through anything."

She gave me an impish grin. "Besides, the twins were starting to think that you didn't like them."

I rolled my eyes at that. "If you only knew how hard it's been not to... But what about Lai? How is she going to feel about all this?"

Jessie laughed. "Lai is all excited about it. Marcus and I discussed it with her yesterday, and she is eager to try you."

Jessie giggled again. "She keeps asking how good you are in bed."

Now my daddy raised a fool, but not a total idiot. I gave in and went along with the plan. I'm not as young as I used to be, but I make up for a lot with experience.

That night, Lai joined us in bed while the twins entertained Marcus. She left very happy in the morning. I was flipping exhausted.

The next night was the twins' turn. Once I got used to the fur, (it felt a lot like mink) they felt as human as Jessie and Lai. Cassandra knew of course. I honestly don't think a single thing went on anywhere in the house that she didn't know about.

"You are adapting to our world better than you think." She told me at breakfast one morning. "The Goddess has favored you indeed."

A few mornings later, I was done brushing my teeth. (Another fad that had caught on) when I happened to yawn in front of the mirror to my surprise and shock, I saw sharp, curved fangs extend down, then retract.

I went to show Jessie. Jessie ran to get Ranal and Cassandra. Ranal was shocked too. But Cassandra was calm. She had been expecting something like this. "The Goddess told me that you would become fully of this world." was all she would say.

Shortly after that, I noticed my hair and beard growing back in their original blonde and red. Hey, this might not be so bad after all. I thought. Finally the day that I was waiting for arrived. The new troops were trained to a fine edge, and the enemy was right where I wanted him.

Marcus and I took the troops out and split them into 4 squads, just like in training.

Jessie stayed home with Lai and the twins, though they weren't happy about it.

The virtues of cleanliness showed when our scouts reported that they could smell the stench of the mercenaries a good half mile away when the wind was right,

Guided by one of our best scouts I surveyed the mercenary camp from the top of a nearby hill with my binoculars. The enemy camp was no longer the sprawling, haphazard mess it had been before. This was good for us, it meant that they were coming together as a cohesive unit, and therefore easier to take the leaders out since they were pretty much gathered in one place.

And their horses were gathered in 4 separate herds on different sides of the camp. I eased back down the hill and rode back to talk to Marcus.

"There are almost 4 thousand of them." I told him. "But they made a couple of bad mistakes."

Marcus looked worried. "But there are only 40 of us. We don't stand a chance against that many men."

"Marcus, think!" I scolded. "Of course, in a fixed battle they'd have our asses for lunch."
A couple of the non-coms snickered.

"But," I continued, "we aren't going to fight them in a stand up battle. Hit and git, remember?"

I laid out a piece of paper and outlined the general area. I marked in where the camp was, where the commanders tents were in the camp, and most importantly for tonight, where the horses were. "Marcus, send each squad out to take out the sentries nearest the horse herds. Take out the guards watching the herds as well. Then herd the horses, slowly, dead away from the camp. East and West herds turn north as soon as you pass this line of hills. North herd travel about 5 miles, then stop and wait for the others. South herd, drive due south for at least 5 miles, then swing west. The main herd will join you at the Forel River at the big horseshoe bend."

One of the non-coms spat. "I thought we were going to kill the bastards, not become horse thieves."

One of the other non-coms smacked the dissenter upside the head. "Fool!" he snarled. "Don't you remember your tactics lessons? Disrupt their transportation. Besides, how well do you think these cavalry troops are going to fight once we set them afoot and they have to walk a few dozen miles to their next battle?"
I marked the man for promotion, provided of course, that he survived the night's activities.

Since the troops were far better trained than I was, I put Marcus in full charge, then sat back and observed.

The sentries and horse guards were taken out with crossbow bolts through the head, or by garrotte. The men eased the horses out and away from the camp, following my directions as best they could. No one raised the alarm, and by dawn, I was with the three combined herds heading towards the Forel River.

A few scouts left behind on fast horses caught up to us about noon. "They are running around confused and angry." laughed one of the scouts. "When we left, they still hadn't sorted things out."

I turned in the saddle and waved at Marcus to close up and ride beside me. "They are not entirely stupid." I told him. "They will eventually start following the horse herds. This many animals make a trail a blind man could follow."

Marcus nodded. "I'll take a squad and set up an ambush about an hour shy of where they would have to stop for the night. I'll hit and run, right when they're the most tired."

"Remember, these are horse soldiers, and they won't be able to walk as far as we could." said the scout.

"Good point." grinned Marcus. "Care to join me on our little party?" he asked the scout.

"Yes sir!" said the scout.

Marcus clapped me on the shoulder and peeled off to collect the members of his squad. I dropped back and told the other non-coms to keep the herd moving. I sent riders with a message south to find the other herds to tell them to use a few grenades to lay an ambush for the troops following them, but not to stay themselves. I wanted the herd to keep moving. Marcus and his men joined us around midnight. He was exhausted, but exhilarated as well. "You should have seen it!" Marcus crowed. "We let the vanguard go by, then we hit the ones who carried their supplies. Anyone who had a fancy uniform got shot, and we left after 3 volleys."

"Great job!" I told him. Then I went and personally praised each member of his team. At dawn, I had another squad go set up an ambush, this time where they would stop at a stream to drink and rest.

That squad caught up to us at suppertime. They had one casualty, a trooper who had gotten careless and exposed himself while still in bowshot of the enemy.

I rode off a mile or so to get a recon report from a dragon. It was Skyfire. "The mercenaries are still coming." The dragon said. "But they are getting cautious."

Skyfire actually smiled at me. A truly horrifying sight. "There is a herd of wild cattle a couple of miles north of the main group. If you'd like, I would be happy to stampede the cattle in their direction."

"I love the way you think Skyfire."

The dragon chuckled. "Of course you do. You have a dragon's evil mind yourself from what I've seen."

"I thank you for the compliment." I replied.

Skyfire took off and winged rapidly out of sight. I rode back to the herd. I looked around and found Marcus. I filled him in on what the dragon had planned.

" A dragon's evil mind huh?" Marcus said when I was done. "Yes, that would describe you very well."
When we reached the Forel River, we found the rest of the horses and the other squad waiting for us. After a few hours of rest, I had them start swimming the herd across the river. Once all the horses and men were over, I sent the herd ahead. There was a narrow pass up ahead where we could collapse the nearly vertical cliffs with explosives to close off both ends of the gap. Once trapped in there, killing all of them would be easy. I had the explosives specialists plant their charges of

black powder at both ends of the pass. As soon as the herd had completely passed through the mile long gap, I had them blow the far end of the pass. A wall of debris a good 60 feet high made exit impossible.

I split the men into two groups and sent one up on either side of the pass. Then we waited. About noon on the second day, the ragged and thoroughly pissed off mercenaries followed the tracks of the horse herd into the pass, thinking of nothing but revenge.

As soon as the last of them were inside the kill zone, the troops blew the open end of the pass, filling it with rubble. I had told the men to use bows to save ammunition, since the enemy was trapped and could not get away. Still, a few gunshots rang out as sharpshooters picked off the mercenaries who had the presence of mind to try to climb the piles of rubble blocking the exits.

Screams and pleas for mercy echoed up from below, but the men had all seen the aftermath of the mercenaries' visits to the local towns. And many had lost family or loved ones.

When everything was quiet below, I sent for wagons to bring barrels of crude oil and alcohol. The crude oil came from surface seeps a days travel away.

For 3 days after the wagons arrived, we poured the barrels of oil down onto the pile of dead and wounded below. With a steady stream of wagons bringing oil to both sides of the pass, we soon had everything below covered in a thick coat of oil. Then the men heaved the alcohol barrels down into the canyon to burst on the rocks and corpses below.

Finally, Marcus and I moved the men back. At a signal, both of us threw torches into the opposite ends of the canyon. The fire caught with a WHOOSH! and the flames nearly singed our heads off!

The fire burned for a full day, sending towering clouds of black, stinking smoke into the sky that could be seen for dozens of miles in all directions.

When the fires died, and the smoke cleared, Marcus sent word out for work crews to come and clear the piles of rubble away so that the pass could be used again.

The pay was the horses that we had liberated from the mercenaries.

Back at the City, Marcus and I were tired, filthy, and happy as hell to have survived. We had lost only 3 men. The one who had been foolish and got an arrow through his guts, and 2 that had fallen into the canyon in their eagerness to kill the enemy.

Marcus was quiet all the way home. This was his first major battle, and he had rappelled down into the canyon after the fires had died to look around. "Like a scene from hell's worst nightmares." Marcus had said when he climbed back up. He had then walked away and threw up everything her had eaten for the last day or so.

I had been down there too. Little was left of the mercenaries but half melted weapons, charred pieces of bone, and odds and ends of metals that had melted and flowed together. I figured it to be the gold and silver they wore and carried as money. “Let the clean up crews have what they could find." I had ordered.

King Jules was ecstatic that we had rid his lands of the mercenary army, But his happiness was tempered by the fact that we still didn’t know who had been pulling the mercenaries strings. Or why.

As for myself, I was just glad that we had gotten away with so few casualties on our side.

Marcus allowed the men a few days to rest and celebrate, then sent out patrols to look for any mercenaries who had deserted or had been stragglers when the main group had been wiped out.

Marcus burst into the bedroom where I was busy trying to keep up with three girls at once.

“Bill, we have a problem!’ he said. “When one of our patrols was a week overdue, we sent another squad out to look for them. Only one man came back, and I doubt that he’ll live through the night.”

“Shit!” I said, “Sorry ladies, but I have to take care of this.”

My wife sat up and reached for her clothes. “We’re coming with you.”

Marcus waited impatiently for us to finish dressing, then led the way downstairs to the main hall where the wounded man was being cared for by Cassandra.

As soon as he caught sight of me, the man raised his head and started talking. “We found Kerin’s squad on our third day out,.” He paused to take a couple of painful breaths. “They were all dead. The only way we knew it was them was by what was left of their armor and equipment. Everything else was burned to ashes."

Suddenly the man stopped talking. His eyes bulged and his back arched until only his head and heels touched the floor. Marcus grabbed his mother and yanked her to the side just in time as the man burst into eye searing flame. When the flash of light died away, nothing was left of the poor man but a pile of ashes lying on the flagstone floor.

Cassandra looked up at me with her eyes wide. "She's back." Was all she said before she fainted.

"Who's back?" I asked.

Jessie was pale as a ghost, and had to try several times to get the words out. "My sister." She said at last, then buried her face against my chest and started to cry.
Marcus stood there looking at the ashes that had once been a friend, and cursed in a low monotone.

I looked up and saw the catkin twins watching from the staircase. "Find Ranal, and tell him to get the king somewhere safe." They nodded and took off at a dead run,

I tightened my hold on Jessie.

Someone was gonna pay.